OUT OF THIS WORLD

Little Laureates

Edited By Kelly Reeves

First published in Great Britain in 2020 by:

Young Writers
Remus House
Coltsfoot Drive
Peterborough
PE2 9BF
Telephone: 01733 890066
Website: www.youngwriters.co.uk

Book Design by Ashley Janson

Softback ISBN 978-1-83928-833-3

Printed and bound in the UK by BookPrintingUK
Website: www.bookprintinguk.com
YB0445H

FOREWORD

Here at Young Writers our defining aim is to promote the joys of reading and writing to children and young adults and we are committed to nurturing the creative talents of the next generation. By allowing them to see their own work in print we believe their confidence and love of creative writing will grow.

Out Of This World is our latest fantastic competition, specifically designed to encourage the writing skills of primary school children through the medium of poetry. From the high quality of entries received, it is clear that it really captured the imagination of all involved.

We are proud to present the resulting collection of poems that we are sure will amuse and inspire.

An absorbing insight into the imagination and thoughts of the young, we hope you will agree that this fantastic anthology is one to delight the whole family again and again.

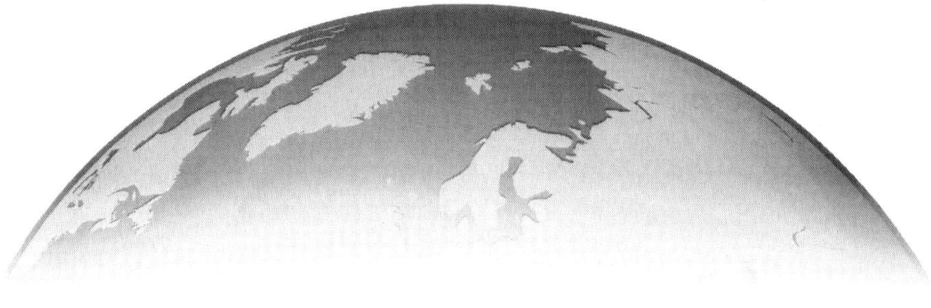

CONTENTS

THE POEMS

On The Ball City

Football is a game of two halves,
Play it with friends and have lots of laughs,
My home team is Norwich City,
Their fan chants are very witty,
We're in the Premier League and hoping not to leave,
Yellow and green make the perfect team,
Captain Canary, makes the fans go lairy,
My favourite player is Buendia, in my opinion, he's the best,
Head and shoulders above the rest,
He comes from Argentina, located in the west,
The game is scrutinised by VAR,
Which many supporters find bizarre,
Two teams of eleven make ninety minutes of football heaven,
Carrow Road is the home of the team,
That are living the dream,
On the ball City!

Darcy James Broughton (9)
Hainford VC Primary School, Hainford

The Competition

There once was a girl named Rubi,
Her parents were very poor,
She had no siblings, no friends to play with,
So she was mostly bored,
Her grandpa was rich and had lots of money,
And went on holidays,
So when they came to see him,
They cancelled 'cause he was away,
One Christmas, they were opening presents,
Getting things they already had,
But one amazing present Rubi got,
Was an incredible brand-new iPad!
The iPad was from Grandpa,
Who is rich as you already know,
He said he had millions upon millions at his house,
Placed neatly all in a row,
Rubi loved this iPad so very much,
She played on it every day,
When she went to school every week,
All she could think about was the game she liked to play,

One day when she got home from school,
She saw a peculiar thing,
On her iPad, it had an ad,
And it made her joyful heart sing!
On the competition,
She could win one million pounds,
Also on her iPad, there's something that she found,
It said to enter,
You have to type your name,
And if you're the one that's chosen,
Then you have won the whole game!
Rubi was thrilled!
As a smile appeared on her face,
She dashed downstairs,
Like she was winning a race!
Well, she was winning the race,
Until she started to lose,
She fell downstairs,
And now, she had a big bruise,
The bruise really hurt,
But Rubi didn't care,
She ran through the corridor,

With the flick of her hair!
She sprinted into the kitchen,
To see her mum and dad,
And when she told them,
They were very glad!
"Rubi, Rubi, that's amazing!
Where did you find that?"
"Oh Mum and Dad, I know it is,
I found it on my brand-new iPad!"
Her mum and dad told her to enter,
To win one million pounds,
Rubi entered the competition,
And felt so very proud,
One week later on her iPad,
As usual, it's the same,
Something popped up about the competition,
Saying she had won the whole game!
Rubi was shocked, and stared at the screen,
She didn't know what to say,
She had a brilliant idea to spend the money,
It was to go on holiday,
Rubi ran out of her room,

To tell her mum and dad,
And when she showed them,
They just stared right at the ad,
They were looking at something,
"Erm, Rubi..." said Dad
"Yes, what's the matter?"
"I'm really sorry, but this might make you a bit sad
The competition is for twelve and over,
But Rubi, you're not that age."
Rubi was shocked about this,
And suddenly went into a rage,
She ran to her bedroom,
"Nothing's ever fair!"
She slammed the door shut,
Without a care,
One hour later, she had time to think,
In her bedroom, all alone,
That maybe her behaviour,
Her mum and dad wouldn't condone,
Because in that moment, Rubi realised,
That love was all you need,

She flew downstairs to hug her mum and dad,
And that was the greatest thing indeed.

Alannah Chudley (10)

Hainford VC Primary School, Hainford

My Wish Upon A Star

I wish I had a magical pet llama,
Twinkling in the moonlight,

I wish I had a magical pet llama,
That would munch on crisp grass.

I wish I had a magical pet llama,
Sparkling like a shell.

I wish I had a magical pet llama,
Flying like a shooting star.

I wish I had a magical pet llama,
With wings shining like a fairy.

I wish I had a magical pet llama,
As playful as can be.

My magical pet llama,
If I wish upon a star tonight, it might come true!

Elsa Jackson (8)
Hainford VC Primary School, Hainford

Tiger The Biggest Cat

Once I was walking in a land far away
With a tiger whose roar
Could be heard from a mile away
He was big and strong
And eleven-feet long
From his head to his tail
He chuffed along to my song
Because he was happy.

His white belly and black and orange stripes
Hid him in the grass
But it was too hot to hunt
So he let the other animals pass.

To cool down, we went for a swim
We swam over three and a half miles
And it was hard to keep up with him.

Gabriel Spencer-Bird (10)
Hainford VC Primary School, Hainford

The Alien And The Chips

There once was a little alien from Mars,
He came to Earth for some chocolate bars,
He flew down to Earth in his tiny ship,
And landed right near a pack of chips,
He grabbed a warm, golden chip,
And ate it in his bright, tiny ship,
He ate it super, super quick,
Then gave the rest a little lick,
He looked around for a chocolate bar,
He looked in a puddle and noticed a star,
He jumped in his ship with chocolate bars,
He was going to fly back to Planet Mars.

Erin Banham-Crooks (10)
Hainford VC Primary School, Hainford

My Dog Cookie

I have a dog called Cookie
She likes to act silly with her best friend, Bailey
When she's silly, she is very clumsy
When she goes on a walk, she is very fast and never comes last
When she sees Bailey, they behave like babies
They roll around on the ground, tumble, stumble and race around
They dig a hole like a mole
When they're in the bath, they get very clean
Only to get dirty again
I have a dog called Cookie
Who I love so, so very much.

Grace Jackson (8)
Hainford VC Primary School, Hainford

My Dream...

I am a mermaid named Sally Surprise
I like to eat cheeseburgers and fries!
Every day, I ride my llama
Then I shout, "I don't need no drama, Mama!"

I woke up
Then my dog came and said, "What's up?"
He started to rap
He was wearing a cool cap.

Then he left the room
With a bim, bam, boom!
So every night, I make a wish,
That there will be a cheeseburger fish!

Chloe Louise Jarrett (10)
Hainford VC Primary School, Hainford

Four Seasons

Spring, baby animals born,
Butterflies and flowers wherever you look,
Children playing outside.

Summer, warm every day
Beaches with children
Building sandcastles and laughing.

Autumn, leaves falling
Days are turning colder,
Children jumping in piles of leaves.

Winter, sun disappears
Days darken, children build snowmen
And make snowballs.

Matilda Price (9)
Hainford VC Primary School, Hainford

I Am Me

I like Christmas Day
I like snow
I like crunchy autumn leaves when they blow.

I like biscuits
I like cake
I like toast when I wake.

I like reading
I like space
I like planets, they are really ace.

I like Mum
I like Dad
I like that sometimes, Mum acts mad.

I like sleeping
I like to dream
When I wake, I can be mean.

Alfie Marchant (10)
Hainford VC Primary School, Hainford

Emotions

Sad, sad, sad
My life on Earth is bad.

Disgust, disgust, disgust
That horrible old rust.

Depressed, depressed, depressed
I'll never be the best.

Fun, fun, fun
Bathing under the sun.

Happy, happy, happy
Always, I am yappy.

Jolly, jolly, jolly
I play with my friend, Olly.

Emotion, emotion, emotion.

Eloise Edridge (11)
Hainford VC Primary School, Hainford

In Space

Space is dark, cold and full with wonder,
There is lightning but no thunder,
A ring around yellow Saturn
The stars make a funny pattern
As the twinkling stars
Make a circle around Mars
When we went for a zoom
We saw an alien, it was blue
In space, there are no trees
No plants and no bees.

Amelia Banham-Crooks (8)
Hainford VC Primary School, Hainford

Fortnite

When I woke up
I prayed for luck
I went to the kitchen
And drank a chug jug
I did ten hours hard work every day
It was children's job to play video games
There was a saying that made me stronger
'Only practice makes perfect'
That saying made my life feel stronger.

Finley Pamment (11)
Hainford VC Primary School, Hainford

Ethan

E is for Earth, beautiful, big, blue planet
T is for the sun, burning bright all day long
H is for hydrogen, hydrating humans
A is for astronomy, study of stars, moon and planets
N is for Neptune, wildly windy, cold as ice.

Ethan Legrice (9)
Hainford VC Primary School, Hainford

The Beach

Waves dancing, full of glee
As if they're calling
Look at me!
Cheeky seagulls
Overhead
Taking people's chips and bread
Troublesome seagulls, "Go to bed!"

Thomas Blackman (11)
Hainford VC Primary School, Hainford

The Purple Cow And The Blue Frog

I am a purple cow
Every time, I go meow
But I don't know how
... to moo!

I am a blue frog
But I think I am a dog
I bark at a log
Woof!

Merryn Britcher (8)
Hainford VC Primary School, Hainford

A Mysterious Door

I see a door
Should I open it?
Okay, I will!
Inside the door
It is invaded with ice
Canopies of frozen air above
Bang!
The door shut behind me
Oh no!
The ice was covering up the door
I looked at my feet
It was covering me up as well!

Darcey Elizabeth Wealthall (10)
Janet Duke Primary School, Laindon

Janet's Jungle Creature

Far upon a time
In a strange, but wacky universe,
Sits a... Belafant!

It has
One beady, little eye,
One venom-filled trunk,
Two hammer-like ears and
A poisonous snow tail.

It lives in
A gold-filled log,
Rats nibble at it.

Evie Dudley (10)
Janet Duke Primary School, Laindon

She Stands Alone

Alone she walks to school every day
Wishing someone would ask to play
She's different you see, they call her the geek
But really, she's only timid and meek.

Alone she stands each day at break
Just wishing one friend she could make
She's different you see, they call her a freak
But they don't know, she's timid and meek.

Alone she goes to lunch to eat
Wishing someone would give her a seat
She's different you see, they call her weird
But they don't know she's not to be feared.

Alone she cries each day at school
Wishing they could think her cool
But she really is no different to you and me
She just needs a friend that will help her, you see.

A smile or a nod is all that it takes
To make someone's day, is no big shakes

Be kind to each other as you don't really know
If someone is sad and feels really low.

So a word of advice, try it and see
It will make you feel good, take it from me
It's nice to be nice, to be helpful and kind
To respect one another makes you happy you'll find.

Milly McIntosh (10)

Kintore Primary School, Kintore

The Sad Earth

If you look outside of the window,
You might see lots of things that grow,
You might see colourful flowers and trees,
Maybe you'll see singing birds and bees.

But all is not like this in other places,
Sometimes people struggle to find their spaces,
And it's not just people, it is animals too,
Some things have life worse than you.

Animals are poached for fur and meat,
Some homeless people have to lie on the streets,
The icebergs are melting and trees are chopped down,
Some humans are mean and boss people around.

Bombs go off and people kill each other,
Guns go boom and it hurts one another,
Drought dries up streams and rivers,
Pollution affects the ocean swimmers.

All of these things are caused by man,
And if we don't stop, the Earth will collapse,
So everyone, don't waste and litter,
To help the world be so much better.

Grace Marshall (11)
Kintore Primary School, Kintore

I Saw A Ghost Eating Toast

When day was night, I got a fright
I saw a ghost, eating toast
It loudly screamed while the moonlight beamed
We both got a scare but I couldn't bear
The way the ghost was eating toast!
It gobbled it down, then the ghost had a frown
For the ghost had finished his toast
He sobbed with despair
Then the ghost screamed, "It isn't fair!"
I asked him why
Then he started to cry
And he said, "I bought some toast
And I liked it the most
But the toast couldn't stay under my command
I wish I had money to buy my own land."
So I said I would help
And the ghost gave a yelp

That night is the one I would always remember
Even on the 15th of September
Because I saw a ghost, eating toast.

Sophia Hulse (8)
Kintore Primary School, Kintore

Unicorns

Unicorns are so magical like fairies
In Unicorn Land, ghosts are very scary
Unicorns are like, the best,
Mermaids wear purple and green shiny vests
In that land, there are a lot of sweets
And magical singers clap the beat
Unicorn are so pretty
The most popular place is Unicorn City
All unicorns have white fur and they each have a cutie mark
There are candy trees with gummies, no bark
The water feels like melted chocolate
All fairies have a secret locket
That world sparkles like the sun
Pink elephants like to run
The stars twinkle high in the sky
And when people come to visit
They always say, "Hey, unicorns can fly!"
Unicorns love to say bye when someone leaves.

Annalise Nicoll (8)
Kintore Primary School, Kintore

Family Fun

Dad is off and so is Mum
I just can't wait to have family fun.

We will go swimming and tumble and glide
Come on Dad, let's go down the slide!

Isla and Mum are splashing around
Oh my goodness, what is that sound?

The wave machine is really so loud
It is really busy and making a crowd.

It's time for lunch,
I think I'll have a cheeseburger, *munch munch munch!*

It's time to go home and watch a movie
I hope it is very groovy.

Movie nights are the best by far
Watching James Bond in his fast car.

Mum, Dad, Isla and me
Having fun as a family!

Adam Gibson (9)
Kintore Primary School, Kintore

Magnificent In Splendour Rise

In a cave far away
Big, bright blue eyes come out to play,
A twig has snapped, birds fly and make a sound
Giving away her hunting ground,
A creature, magnificent in splendour rise
A teacher, a hunter, an animal with pride.

Up high on the mountainside, camouflaged by rocks
Stealthily watching mountain goats, the prey that she stalks,
Sunrise happens, a figure standing high
Thinking, am I ready to chase and try?
Blood and flesh on the ground, all is silent
Except one sound...

Ally Peter (10)
Kintore Primary School, Kintore

The Lost Alien

Far away in big, black space
An abandoned planet, a lonely place
A little green alien,
One of a kind, wondering in his mind,
"Where is my sister? Where is my dad?
I feel rather bad."

A little green alien,
Being cautious of the future ahead,
Thinking of further dread,
What is he to do?
As he thought and thought,
He did a lot and a lot,
And time was bought and bought,
Far away in big, black space,
An abandoned planet, a lonely place...

Janvi Ashara (10)
Kintore Primary School, Kintore

The Sun, The Moon And The Stars

The sun produces heat
It helps grow food for us to eat
Like vegetables, fruit, berries and wheat
Cows eat grass to give us milk and meat.

The moon is bright and the sun shines light
At the end of the day
The sun goes away
And the moon comes out for night.

I like to look up at the stars in the sky
Way up high
They make me wish I could fly.

Stars are balls of gas
They sparkle like glass
And I like it when shooting stars pass.

Cara Peacock (8)
Kintore Primary School, Kintore

There's A Dinosaur Outside!

There's a dinosaur outside!
It's green and possibly mean,
It's bigger than me and it's gonna eat me,
It's scarier than a bee.

There's a dinosaur outside!
It may have travelled far through time,
It ate some candy, worth less than a dime,
But now I can't think of a rhyme.

There's a dinosaur outside!
It has teeth as sharp as icicles,
It almost stole my bicycle,
And I'll be stuck with a tricycle.

William Grant (9)
Kintore Primary School, Kintore

Unicorn Lake

People shall say it's fake
Yes, Unicorn Lake
The lake is mystical and true
Say bib-a-bob-a-boo shall-a-ca-doo
And a unicorn shall appear for you!

It can be black, pink, blue or white
Really any colour you like!
It can eat sweets, broccoli, carrots and meats!
It could have fluffy hair down or even in pleats.

So if you like magic and myths and think they are true...
Then Unicorn Lake is the place for you!

Jack Burton Hayfield (10)
Kintore Primary School, Kintore

Who Cares?

Sometimes you feel,
Like you're not there,
Cold and isolated and full of despair,
Everyone looks and everyone stares,
Everyone but one, does not care,
And this individual gives you praise,
For everything you dare to do,
they'll be there,
Standing beside you,
Whether it's a handshake or an earthquake,
But keep in mind,
She's there, she cares.

Amy Cumming (10)
Kintore Primary School, Kintore

Zapple Came To Earth

Zapple was an alien who lived on planet Zalien
His hair was as dark as the night sky
He was as green as grass
Flying through the universe
He missed the brake and hit reverse
Landing here on Planet Earth
When he saw what we had done
With rising seas and burning trees
He got back in his rocket ship
Blasted off and got out quick
Because the Earth seemed very sick.

Grace Smith (8)
Kintore Primary School, Kintore

Friendship Forever

I love my friends, I don't want it to ever end
I love my friends, we love to share
We play around like we just don't care
At school or at our homes, I'm sure some of my friends have funny bones
We laugh, we giggle, we share our pencils from Smiggle
We giggle, we gaggle all night long
This could be our friendship song.

Indee Calder (8)
Kintore Primary School, Kintore

Titanic

The boat was called Titanic,
And everyone was in a panic,
As the tragedy began,
Rose and Jack had a plan,
The Titanic was old,
Because it was a long time ago,
They all thought they would need to row,
Through the cold sea and show,
Oh, what a terrible blow,
A horrible history it was.

Erin Rainnie (8)
Kintore Primary School, Kintore

Colours Of Africa

Endless beauty to behold
Africa's colours are big and bold.

Horizons of orange and red
Rolling mountains widely spread.

Hills of green and seas of blue
Sunsets of pink and purple too.

Africa's more beautiful than I can say
Where rhinos roam and children play.

Keegan Bingham (7)
Kintore Primary School, Kintore

Flower Of Spring

Flowers growing from the ground
Birds chirping all around
People walking on the path
Basket of flowers in their hand
Church bells ringing and people singing
Egg hunting and flower painting
Lambs being born in fields
So fuzzy and soft to feel.

Sophie Birkett (9)
Kintore Primary School, Kintore

The Fascinating Planets

The bright sun
Weighs a ton
When I look at the stars
I can sometimes see Mars
Jupiter is so big
But it weighs no more than a fig
When it is a blood-wolf moon
I listen to my favourite tune
Now I'm done
You go have some fun.

Andrew Walker (8)
Kintore Primary School, Kintore

Winter

Winter swirled
Through the frosted, swaying trees
She sprinkled snow to make everything
As pure and as glimmering as freshly-sliced diamonds
Winter spun with dancing snowflakes
She spread Christmas joy and love.

Winter's eyes
Glimmered with a touch of hope
She snuggled in her beautiful ivory snow blanket
She gleamed with the lustre of a pearl.

Winter
Delicately and only the wind heard her
Winter's voice was a song
The ocean rowed to the rhythm.

Winter is warmth
Her heart creates life, giving fire she is
The hold of hot hands
The comforting duvet around a cold child
Bubbling hot chocolate

Snuggly hugs from your mother to soothe you
She is love.

Winter designs
Light, she hushed every furry bear to their cave
She sang a lullaby to landscapes of snowy owls
and singing robins
She twirled, swirled, danced merrily
With her single flame lantern.

Winter hopes
For people to dream
Her crystal heart had shattered
It was the sun's beam
But she left her magical fairy kingdom.

Hannah Keen (7)
Lady Joanna Thornhill (Endowed) Primary School, Wye

The Poison Beast

Poison Beast, Poison Beast
If it sees you, you'll be its next feast
Digs his claws in your body
It's his favourite hobby
Purple body, sharp silver claws,
Red spiky spines when he kills you
You can't get an alibi
Crushing worlds with extreme ease
Making people beg on their knees
Gobbling everything in sight
You won't survive its ghoulish bite
Quick as a cheetah, stronger than an ox
Stealthier than a lion, he can even break a lock
Sleeps in a crater in the dark night
He catches his prey
His habitat is the island beyond even Earth
And that is his own turf
Circles the Earth, over and over
Going so fast, he's like a supernova.

Joe Hussell (10)
Lady Joanna Thornhill (Endowed) Primary School, Wye

Lottie Salkeld's Ice Cream Store

I am Lottie Salkeld
I run Salkeld's Ice Cream Store
Do yourself a favour and try the flavours on my list.

Hot chocolate brownie ice cream
Warm hot chocolate honeycomb dream
Cotton candy cookie bake
Cotton candy chocolate cake
Brownie cookie candy cane crush
Yummy chocolate honeycomb blush
Yummy brownie cookie cake
Chocolate chip ice cream, cream cake
Delicious cookie brownie bake
Chocolate cookie brownie cake.

I am Lottie Salkeld
I run Salkeld's Ice Cream Store
Come inside and try my list
And then you'll surely ask for more.

Lottie Arrandale-Salkeld (8)
Lady Joanna Thornhill (Endowed) Primary School, Wye

Mythical Creature

Silver and gold constellations,
Paint the night sky with warm sensations,
Gold, bright stars build up to form,
A beautiful creature by dawn,
Falling down from the dark space,
Fast enough to win a race,
Landing in the sapphire sea,
Further than your eyes can see,
Even longer than you can run,
Even brighter than the sun,
Yet tinier than my tippy toe,
As colourful as the rainbow,
Ruby-red,
Yellow too,
Grassy-green,
Baby-blue,
Rosy-pink,
Chestnut-brown,
Grey like a sink,
That's all I found.

Sofia Shahsavari (10)
Lady Joanna Thornhill (Endowed) Primary School, Wye

The Wild Cauldron

Like flaming fire,
Like midnight
Unheard footsteps into the deep, dark cave.

A barking cauldron as wild as can be
With a whizz, pop, bang!
Like lava, the cauldron frothed
And the spell was done.

Like deadly death
A nose like icicles
The unheard footsteps returned
The wizard's work was done.

Back at home, the wizard looked at her watch
And said to herself, "Georgina, you're late for school!

So off she went, skipping like a lamb in spring
Her wild dog following behind.

Freddy Kyrke-Smith (8)
Lady Joanna Thornhill (Endowed) Primary School, Wye

Annie Carvill's Ice Cream Store

I am Annie Carvill,
I run Carvill's Ice Cream Store
Taste a flavour from my freezer,
You'll surely ask for more.
Lots of different flavours in my freezer,
Pick one that you like!

Flavours:
Chocolate doughnut sprinkle
Yummy perry-winkle
Golden syrup Spam
Juicy watermelon ham
Strawberry curry biryani
Raspberry fruit salami
Pickly cookie pancake cluster
Warm hot chocolate lava buster
No mice
Eat it with ice.

Thank you for trying my ice cream,
Make sure you eat it nicely.

Annie Carvill (9)

Lady Joanna Thornhill (Endowed) Primary School, Wye

Dawkins' Ice Cream Store

I am Ruth Dawkins
I run Dawkins' Ice Cream Store
Put your fork in
And try some more flavours on my menu.

Macaroni bubblegum
Banana split plum
Tomato cheese taco
Vegetable stew on-the-go
Pizza pasta bake
Pringles kiwi shake
Crispy apple pear
Pepper chocolate dare
Ice chilli banoffee
Chilli cheese toffee.

I am Ruth Dawkins
I run Dawkins' Ice Cream Store
Sorry all my flavours have gone out the door!

Ruth Victoria Dawkins (9)
Lady Joanna Thornhill (Endowed) Primary School, Wye

My Sister Elodie

I love my sister, Elodie
I'm going to miss her when she goes
She's like a second mum to me
I keep her on her toes
She teaches me all the dance moves to our favourite songs
It won't be the same when she's at uni
I'll miss her so much!

We love doing art together
It's our favourite thing to do
What am I going to do without her?
If you knew her, you would miss her too!

Amelie Reid-Williams (7)
Lady Joanna Thornhill (Endowed) Primary School, Wye

In Spring

The crisp morning air swishes, swishes
As sheep mothers are getting their wishes
Lambs skip and prance
While trees sway and dance
Spring flowers are coming out
Winter flowers are starting to pout
Blossom trees are growing more
Fluffy clouds are going to pour
Magic is in the air
Flowers are starting to flare
Crows are peeping out, mild and meek
The sun is playing hide-and-seek.

Bella Snart (10)
Lady Joanna Thornhill (Endowed) Primary School, Wye

Enchanted Forest

I'm spinning around
In the ever enchanted forest
Spooky, jolly, mixed emotions
The trees were praying for sunlight
It was the dead of night
My courage was fading
In the ever enchanted forest
The birds were singing
The trees were clinging onto night
For I was in the ever enchanted forest!

Grace Anderson (10)
Lady Joanna Thornhill (Endowed) Primary School, Wye

Princess Pug

There was once a pug
She was very smug.

She wore a crown
And she never felt down.

She loved pink
But once drank a really magical drink.

The drink was strong
And the magic would not stay for long.

She started feeling light
Like she would fly through the night.

Florence Alves (10)
Lady Joanna Thornhill (Endowed) Primary School, Wye

The Enchanted Forest

In the enchanted forest
Lives a beautiful florist
The magical bells ring
And the sweet birds sing
Vines with juniper leaves
Dancing fairies for those who believe
Dazzling stars shining bright
In the darkness of the night
In the enchanted forest,
Lives a beautiful florist!

Sophie Maxfield (9)
Lady Joanna Thornhill (Endowed) Primary School, Wye

Little Red Heart

I grow on a farm,
But you can grow me at home.
You can pick your own,
Pick me when I'm red,
And not when I'm green.
I taste delicious,
With yummy cream.
I am juicy like an orange.
I have bumpy seeds but no hair.
What am I?

Answer: A strawberry.

Isla Wallis (8)
Lady Joanna Thornhill (Endowed) Primary School, Wye

Witches And Wizards

With an evil cackle in the night
She will give you and me a fright!
But there is a wizard in the land,
Who will always give you a helping hand,
He is loving, he is kind,
And has happy eyes,
The witch though is deadly and dangerous
Has no pride with all that, she never dies.

Lucy Hendrick (9)
Lady Joanna Thornhill (Endowed) Primary School, Wye

Mystery Magic

Mystery magic
It may be tragic
It may be good or bad.

Mystery magic
It may be tragic
It may be very sad.

Mystery magic
It may be tragic
It may be hot or cold.

Mystery magic
It may be tragic
It may be very bold.

Ellie Taylor (9)
Lady Joanna Thornhill (Endowed) Primary School, Wye

Space

Space the human front has combined
The sun has turned to a face of yellow
She disappears at the amplest of times
And the sun was but a chin of gold
And certainly, her way might pass

Mars the human demon of light
He lies by dripping blood drops of rain
And red-faced god of war descended, arid
He roars when the wind roars at night
And the most like a demon I've ever known

Saturn, your misty rings like ghost skirts
Your airless manned sculpture of a face
Has turned cheek to cheek
Advanced to a human-like space
Her ring is an engagement to your life

Earth, your misty gaps leave life in your space
He cries the waters to show how much he cares
His friends are the continents
And delighted by the fact they're on Earth
Your bizarre light reproduces animals and humans every day.

Amy Holmes (10)
Lawford CE (VA) Primary School, Lawford

Space

Some of our planets are fiery
Some of our planets are spinning
They're unexplored selves stay there
All day

Venus as a fiery type
Her body, fierce red
Her eyes as hard as ice
Her lips as red as gold

Saturn is a cold type
Her body, ice-cold
Her eyes as blue as ice
Her lips as light as gas

Mars is a blue type
Her body as hard as rock
Her eyes are hard as rock
Her lips as rocky as the moon

The sun is a hot type
Her body as hot as any gas

Her eyes as yellow as fire
Her lips as fiery as a monkey

The moon is a light type
Her body as revolting as a sun
Her eyes are filled with gas

Earth is our planet
Her body is blue and white
Her eyes are blue as water
Her lips as white as a chicken

Mercury has a fiery, frozen face
That is airless, its face a rocky type
That is a lifeless shape

Her forehead, hopeless grey
Her cheek as hard as a rock
Her body, doomed green

Her lips as revolting as a sun
But what must be a rock
That never grows upon the world
Below it.

Summer Smith (9)
Lawford CE (VA) Primary School, Lawford

Space, A Final Frontier

Space, a final frontier like the men
Which were sent to discover beyond Earth

Mars with volcanoes like their mum exploding
With blood mixed with mud the size of spuds

Earth, goddess with silver hair and silver shoes
Who will she choose to fit her shoes?

Saturn with misty rings like bins
It's like the rings people wear
Pluto's over there

Pluto, like sapphire, also like blue fire
It's also a dwarf planet
A beautiful ice bonnet

Uranus, quite spacious
It's colour, quite turquoise
Like its beautiful eyes
Looking down on you
This planet is not blue!

Neptune is blue, not like you
It does have eyes and no disguise
It likes to stand out like everyone should

Mercury is stone, it doesn't stand out though
But it does have cheeks which peek over its feet

Venus, quite blank, not like a bank
Had money which people pick up using their hands
And Venus has those too.

Daniel Fairweather (9)
Lawford CE (VA) Primary School, Lawford

Space, An Unknown Journey

With his emerald cheeks he shines in the sunlight
And his graceful face, so blue and white
That she glimpses in the night

With his skin as cold as ice and snow
And his eyes ever so grey
He cries tears of ice as he's the furthest away

With his rocky face and silver eyes
And his lips as cold as ice
She shines upon the night and goes away
In the day
With her amber chin and dark skin, she rests

With her ghastly belt and rocky eyes
She looks at Jupiter with despise
And with her unpleasant look
She turns her head and rests her tilted head

With his skin as cold as ever
And his chin like fog and silver

He looks at Neptune with despair
And turns his head back to Jupiter

With his three eyes, he can see
But with two, the other one is spare
In case he goes achoo!
With his auburn curls and red hair
He goes and waits.

Noah Hammond (9)

Lawford CE (VA) Primary School, Lawford

Space

Space, the place we live in
With the stars as a twinkling belt
Their face of silver and their shoes
Their body surrounded by planets

Mars demon-like
With red dropping
Burst tears of red lava
Ares' face from the god of war

Saturn with misty rings like a vast ghost
With a belt or a skirt
His face rocky and as yellow as a buttercup
Right in the middle of all the planets

Neptune, the only planet fully blue
His body is as cool as a fridge
His mouth full of frozen ice
Sapphire, it is

Pluto, the smallest planet of all
Rocks and bumps all around it

Its body as grey as iron
But his mouth is only a small section of it

The moon turns her face
Her eye of amber shines on the sun
Her shoes are the universe
The moon has a chin of gold.

Victoria Kemp (10)
Lawford CE (VA) Primary School, Lawford

The Planets

Space, a place where not many men have gone before
Stars, big dots in the sky like diamonds on the finger of the Earth
Neptune, the furthest planet from the sun, made of ice, blue king of frost

Mars, the Devil, dripping blood drops of rain
Lava tears dropping
Friend of God when he is angry

Mercury, Earth's next-door neighbour
Brown eyes both sides, she loves to say hi to Earth
Most of the time
Her colours are fantastic!
She is the queen of beauty

Venus, colours are like snow and stars
Her eyes are the yellow and the white is her smile
And she smiles at the Earth
She knows we are there

Uranus is a beautiful planet, turquoise colour
Her hat is the stars
She has a minty eye that is on God's nice side.

Aimee Ablett (9)
Lawford CE (VA) Primary School, Lawford

Our Amazing Solar System

The sun is an angry ball of fire
Mercury is a small child
Venus is a beautiful lady
Although it is quite wild

Earth has snow for hair and feet
The moon is its friend
Mars is a desolate place
And that has been penned

Jupiter is incomprehensible
It is the planet's king
Whilst Saturn is the second largest
And its skirt is its ring

Uranus is always lying down
It lives on its head
It's always lying on its side
Although it has no bed

Neptune is shivering all the time
Its ice never melts
It needs a really thick coat
It might not need belts

Our solar system is amazing
It is like a person
With planets as its feelings
As they are all different.

Elizabeth Jordan (10)

Lawford CE (VA) Primary School, Lawford

Space, An Unknown World

Space, an unknown world where many would like to visit but many will never visit.
Mars crying tears of flames as Venus watches over like a parent to a child
Saturn with its ring teaming with a gorgeous aroma
Mercury warming its face up like a cat in the sun
The solar system is a very hostile environment where many amazing things happen a lot and will never be explored
Pluto with his cold surfaces that look like a huge snake has moved around and around the planet
One of the largest planets is Jupiter,
Jupiter is rocky and unexplored and if we explored it, something might fail
We have never lost a man in space and we don't want this to be the first.

Harry Freeman (10)
Lawford CE (VA) Primary School, Lawford

The Wonders Of Space And Planets

Space, the final frontier for man
To discover what lies beyond our planet

Mars, the planet of war
Home to blood and gore
Its bright red clothes
Covered in black-like bones

Earth, Mother Earth
Simple but stern
Orbits and turns
Like a ballerina's skirt

Pluto, smallest planet of them all
And never a friend of Neptune
Who is super, super tall,
So that's our tiny planet
Crowded, rocky and unexplored

The moon, Earth's friend
But sometimes needs a bit of a mend

Wishes he could be planet number nine
Or even King of Valentine.

Fallon Corrigan (10)
Lawford CE (VA) Primary School, Lawford

Autumn

The morning dew and sunkissed grass
The awakening of raindrops shine like glass
The crunch of decaying leaves fall off trees
Twirling and whirling in the autumn breeze
Crackling bonfires exploding with light
Glistening moon and darkening night
Unique colours: gold and brown
Shone and shine like royalty's crown
As Mother Nature begins to fade
The changes of nature begin to be made.

Lacey Purvis (10)
Lew Trenchard Primary School, Lewdown

Orbit My Rabbit

One ear up
One ear down
Orbit is the cutest rabbit in town

Nibble, nibble
Eats anything
Even a magazine

This rabbit has a habit
Jumping on a shelf
Which is not good for her health

In her hutch
Which is shut
She lays and devours
All the flowers.

Charlotte Pickbourne (10)
Lew Trenchard Primary School, Lewdown

Magnitaurs

M agnitaurs are dangerous
A re able to vaporise Earth
G inormous stars
N ever quitting
I n ten thousand years
T remendous stars
A mazing but deadly
U nbelievably powerful
R emarkably blue light
S tars are beautiful.

Jaydon Barr (10)
Lew Trenchard Primary School, Lewdown

Autumn

A utumn breeze blowing leaves off the trees
U nder my feet, the crunching leaves lay decaying on the floor
T orches of light spring with delight
U nique colours like furious fires
M other Nature begins to fade
N uts and berries for wildlife to enjoy.

Katie Mudge (10)
Lew Trenchard Primary School, Lewdown

Fright Night

N ight is creeping
I nto my room
G hastly shadows
H aunt my dreams
T errifying pictures fill
M y head
A s I hide in my bed
R eally terrified
E verything seems unreal
S lowly, I drift off to sleep.

Samuel Wilson (10)
Lew Trenchard Primary School, Lewdown

Nightmares

N aughty and scary
I ntriguing but daring
G hastly and gory
H ardly a story
T ampering with memory
M iraculously shaming
A dmittedly despairing
R udely uncaring
E ndlessly shocking.

Rosie Slocombe (10)
Lew Trenchard Primary School, Lewdown

Sweets

S weets are yummy
W atering in your mouth every second
E very mouthful just gets better
E ven when it's sour
T owering piles
S o delicious.

Logan Starling (9)
Lew Trenchard Primary School, Lewdown

Groovy Greek Gods

Hades
Hades, ruler of the dead
Owned a dog with more than one head
Hades, jealous of Zeus, his brother
Maybe he should be nicer to his mother

Zeus
Zeus was the most powerful of all gods
They didn't like to be called snobs
He was the god of the sky and the king of Olympus
They didn't like it when the mount was called
Mount Yucky

Hestia
Hestia was the goddess of the hearth and home
She didn't like to be in bloom
Hestia, Hestia, brother of Hades
She didn't like other ladies.

Lexie Smith (8)
Mapplewells Primary & Nursery School, Sutton-In-Ashfield

Crystal Maze

Space catches our imagination
Gorgeous like a jar of glitter

Sky above us
Is infinite like friendship
It lasts for as long as possible
Marvellous like a piece of artwork
As beautiful as a princess

Black like a goth's cloak
Silent like the streets at night
It makes me nervous not knowing
What there is still to find

And I exhibit the unknown
Space is black, crystals floating in another world
It's a jar of black glitter
Sometimes the galaxy sky grabs you and pulls you up.

Amelia Rose Cresci (10)
Mapplewells Primary & Nursery School, Sutton-In-Ashfield

Super Space

Space plucks our imagination
A supernova as the big bang
Up above in the supreme sky

As optimistic as the first man on Mars
Glaring as much as a golden bell
As gloomy as the loudest, deepest, darkest
Dungeon in the depths of Hell

As dark blue as the water in the Challenger Deep
I only hear an echo of the Big Bang
Uncomfortable as sitting on rocks

And we will go together
Scout forever until the sun falls tomorrow

Space plucks our imagination
It's a wonderful place!

Oliver Parry (10)
Mapplewells Primary & Nursery School, Sutton-In-Ashfield

Goddess Mighty Athena

Athena, Athena, Athena
She is a goddess of arts and wisdom
Also, her symbol is an owl
She ate jam tarts
Athena, Athena, Athena
She is a daughter of Zeus
Athena drank juice

Athena, Athena, Athena
Strong and brave
Makes a little firework display
She likes to have shepherd's pie
She has big, clanking armour
Also, she did drama

Sheep were in a barn
Athena is a farmer

Athena, Athena, Athena
She is really wise
Athena is really wise.

Sofie Mai Oliver (7)
Mapplewells Primary & Nursery School, Sutton-In-Ashfield

River Racer

A kennings

Rapid river
River-racer
Bubble-maker
Crowded-crasher
Super-slapper
Life-giver
Wild-whoosher
Tarnished-crater
Lifesaver
Rapid-ruler
Clear-crusher
Golden-breaker
Smiling-slapper
Whoosh wider
Violent-thinker
Sloper-looper
Poetry-maker
Dull-whistler
Loud maker
Whistling water

Clever whoosher
Crazy racer
Fast river
Gazing blazer
Noise-creator
Grand river
Rocky ruler
Smashing-speeder
Crowded-whoosher.

Lucy Ann Read (9)
Mapplewells Primary & Nursery School, Sutton-In-Ashfield

The Olympians Of Olympus

Poseidon, the king of the sea
Poseidon holds a trident like me
Poseidon, jealous of his brother
Shouldn't have made the sea from salt but sugar

Zeus, he's the king of gods
Throws lightning, *zap, crash, pow!*
He can turn into animals but his favourite thing to be
Is the eagle that looks like you and me!

Apollo, full of fire and flames
The god of the sun
So shout his name
He pulls the sun along
Yes, he does
That's his job.

Emilia Wright (8)
Mapplewells Primary & Nursery School, Sutton-In-Ashfield

Spectacular Space

Space captures our minds
As gloomy as a rainy day
In the super sky

Immense like marvellous mountains
Stunning space is amazing
As significant as a man on the moon

As dark as a black hole
As silent as the night sky
As queazy as you spinning round in circles

And we marvel at this wonderful world above
Observe the spectacular sights
Settled feelings when you're done

Space captures our minds
Space is a disco ball.

Tia Louise Costello (10)
Mapplewells Primary & Nursery School, Sutton-In-Ashfield

Wondrous Space

Space grapples our imagination
As infinite as time
Above the skies in a whole new world

Gloomy as a cave
Mysterious UFOs soaring through the galaxy
Elegant stars shooting through the galaxy

As black as a pitch-black room
Thunder of rockets heard for blast-off
Low gravity, weightless feelings

And I...
Observe the area
Feel jubilant

Space grapples our imagination
Space is a workshop of infinite mysteries.

Cailen Doud (10)
Mapplewells Primary & Nursery School, Sutton-In-Ashfield

Space Is Controlling Me!

Space controls my mind
An immense as the Eiffel Tower
In the sky, up, up and above is more than your intense
Imagination can think of

Exquisite space is like a jar of glitter
The superior solar system is in my head
I started feeling a bit queasy

And I just realised how different
I thought it would be
Exhibiting useless Uranus
Relieved to see normal life again

Space controls my mind
Space is a magical new world.

Jessica Louise Hayden (9)
Mapplewells Primary & Nursery School, Sutton-In-Ashfield

Space Clutches Our Imagination

Gorgeous like a piece in a castle
Sky above us is as infinite as friendship
Infinite lasts forever like friendship
Marvellous as a piece of art
Nutritious is as delicious as chocolate

Dizzy as a rocky roller coaster
Black as a dark goth
Silent as a mouse on Christmas Eve

And I valued its stars
View the mythical stars in the galaxy

Realised that you didn't get sucked up there
Space is a jar of dancing crystals.

Dylan Pearce (10)
Mapplewells Primary & Nursery School, Sutton-In-Ashfield

Gruesome Gods

Zeus, king of gods, very powerful he was
Throwing lightning through the sky
Crashing high through the sky
His favourite animal flew through the sky

Ares, god of war, be careful, he's cruel
His spear is deathly and shocking
If you went to war, be careful of Ares

Hermes, as quick as a flash
If you went near he might pass
Be careful, he's really fast like a flash
He will send a message really fast.

Blake James Eteson (7)
Mapplewells Primary & Nursery School, Sutton-In-Ashfield

King Of The Gods

Zeus, Zeus, the king of the sky
You better not anger him or you're in for a fight
Bang, bang! Lightning bolts fly
Smashing on the floor, you're in for a fright

Oh, Zeus, Zeus, you're in a state
You better calm down or you'll end up down a hill
He hates mortals, if you see him, you better scream
Run, run!
Zeus, Zeus! *Abonnnng, abonnnng,* a boomerang
Flying through those mortals.

Noah Rossiter (8)
Mapplewells Primary & Nursery School, Sutton-In-Ashfield

Sparkling Space

Space captures your imagination
It is a colossal whale
In the super sky

Gloomy goo
As miniature as Mercury
As glum as Neptune

As black as coal
Silence covers the universe
As dizzy as a hula-hooping person

And I exhibited its wonders
It's a gorgeous place
Bewildered that we're leaving

Space captures your imagination
Space is a colossal whale.

Vienna Harvey (10)
Mapplewells Primary & Nursery School, Sutton-In-Ashfield

Spectacular Space

Space grabs your imagination
As massive as the sun
In the superior sky

As enormous as a skyscraper
Immense as a rock band
As gloomy as a bear's cave

As black as a pen lid
Silent like a cheetah hunting
As nervous as me fighting a bull

And we marvel at the wonderful world
We explore all of the galaxy
And when we come back, we are dizzy with excitement.

Max Hawkins (10)
Mapplewells Primary & Nursery School, Sutton-In-Ashfield

Super Space

Space grabs our minds
As massive as a skyscraper
Up in the sky

Immense like skydiving
Gloomy like bad weather
Fascinating like meeting your favourite celebrity

Black like far off darkness
As silent as night-time
As strange as aliens

And I go across the galaxy
Exploring everything

Space grabs our minds
Space is an endless loop.

Elijah Smith (10)
Mapplewells Primary & Nursery School, Sutton-In-Ashfield

Spectacular Space

Space catches our creativity
As massive as the sun
In the superior sky

Infinite as a computer's database
Silent as a funeral
Nervous as a patient in a hospital

And I observe the gloomy world around me
Exhibit around the enormous galaxy
As dizzy as a child on a roller coaster

Space catches our creativity
Space is a multicoloured disco ball.

Aaron Daniel Spencer (9)
Mapplewells Primary & Nursery School, Sutton-In-Ashfield

The Super Greek Gods

Poseidon, Poseidon
God of the sea
If he gets angry
He will eat you and me
Poseidon, Poseidon
God of the sea
You have a trident
Just like me
Poseidon, Poseidon
God of the sea
He has fish like you
Poseidon, Poseidon
God of the sea
You have a submarine
Just like me
Zeus, Zeus
The king of the sky
I don't even think this rhymes

Tinaya Hardy (7)
Mapplewells Primary & Nursery School, Sutton-In-Ashfield

King Of The Gods

Zeus zapping lightning left and right
He has great might
When he is angry, he zaps lightning

Zeus, Zeus, the king of the gods and the sky
But can only fly as an eagle
He has two brothers, Hades and Poseidon

Zeus, zapping lighting, *bang, bang, pow!*
If it lands next to you, it'll be a fright
If you anger him
He might bite.

Jacob Danby (8)
Mapplewells Primary & Nursery School, Sutton-In-Ashfield

Olympians

Apollo was loved by everyone
So young and yet so wise
Pushing the sun across the sky
Making room for the milky moon

Ares, son of Zeus
He had a queen, savage and mean
Ares, god of war
What was he good for?

Hermes was the messenger god
So fast, sometimes lost
His shoes go *flip, flap, flop*
Speedy shoes are too fast.

Harry Fell (8)
Mapplewells Primary & Nursery School, Sutton-In-Ashfield

Greek Gods Rule Greece

Poseidon, Poseidon, the god of the sea
He has a trident just like me
Any fishermen pass by, not praying to him
They will die just like a fly

Zeus, Zeus, the king of the gods
He is muscley with a lightning bolt
He was very strong, yes he was
And that's all he was
He could throw lightning through the sky
Zap, zap, zap!

Jack Digby (7)
Mapplewells Primary & Nursery School, Sutton-In-Ashfield

Space Catches Our Imagination

As gigantic as the sun
Up above is a wonderful world

I am a colossal asteroid
As spectacular as a rocket
The gloomy, dark space is spectacular

As black as the dark sky
As silent as a whisper
As queazy as a person on a roundabout

And we float around like a bauble
Observe the perfect planets
Space is a mammoth.

Jack Beastall (9)
Mapplewells Primary & Nursery School, Sutton-In-Ashfield

Rivers

R apid rivers dash down the mountains
I n the river, rocks sit and wait for the shiny diamond-like water to splash them
V iolent waves blow bubbles down the serene woodland
E merald trees surround the river, giving out oxygen
R eflecting the blue sky in its crystal-clear water
S loping down as the river falls.

Dylan Hall (9)
Mapplewells Primary & Nursery School, Sutton-In-Ashfield

Poseidon

God of the sea
Sailors would pray
Sailors would be safe to pass
His brother was Zeus the king of all gods

Splish! Splash! Splosh!
Water everywhere!
Water in the sky
His trident is as gold as a pot

Splish! Splash! Splosh!
Beautiful palace under the sea
Power and anger that shook the world.

Harley Colin Beardsley (8)
Mapplewells Primary & Nursery School, Sutton-In-Ashfield

My River Is Slow

M agical wave river in the bushes
Y elling, the river shouts

R acing as slow as a snail
I want to touch it
V ery romantic
E mbraces you
R emember to go to the river

S ays hello
L ife-giver
O pen minds
W aves goodbye.

James Wren (8)
Mapplewells Primary & Nursery School, Sutton-In-Ashfield

Calm And Rapid Rivers

Rapid rivers race
In a big disgrace
There's not a straight line
You can search that online
Rivers can be calm
So they're not disarmed
They can be different shapes
Even like grapes
More than one can be connected
Even dissected into another
This was my rhyme
It took me a lot of time.

Lewis Jones (9)
Mapplewells Primary & Nursery School, Sutton-In-Ashfield

Crystal-Clear River

This river is beautiful
It is as fast as a cheetah in the wild
It is crystal clear and bubbly
And flows through the day and night
It is as shiny as the big blue sky
It flows through the world fast
It's like it is blowing bubbles
And it glimmers in the moonlight.

Felicity Sam (9)
Mapplewells Primary & Nursery School, Sutton-In-Ashfield

The Gods Of Mount Olympus

Zeus, Zeus, the king of the gods
If he gets angry, it will be *boom!*
Zeus, Zeus, he's a volcano erupting

Poseidon, Poseidon, god of the sea
Don't mess with him, I guarantee
Talking to fish like normal
He has a trident, like me.

Daisy Lockley (7)
Mapplewells Primary & Nursery School, Sutton-In-Ashfield

Zeus

The king of the gods with thunder at his side
He has a long, brown beard and beautiful eyes
As blue as the sky

His beautiful, blue blowing balloons
Pam! Pam! Pam! Zeus might be scared sometimes
Zeus might be old and wise.

Joshua Westlake (7)
Mapplewells Primary & Nursery School, Sutton-In-Ashfield

Aphrodite

Beautiful goddess of love
Beautiful eyes and nose
Beautiful daughter of Zeus
Beautiful doves as white as snow
Beautiful swans pulled her through the air
Her hair glows, dazzling like giant stars
Giant stars.

Bethany Darwin (8)
Mapplewells Primary & Nursery School, Sutton-In-Ashfield

Grumpy, Groovy Gods

Hades
God of the dead
He has a dog with three heads
God of the dead
He woke up on the wrong side of the bed

Ares
God of war
He hates to snore
God of war
He wants to break your door.

Alfie Brown (8)
Mapplewells Primary & Nursery School, Sutton-In-Ashfield

Aphrodite

Aphrodite is so beautiful and lovely
She has doves as white as snow
They pulled her in her chariot
With a mighty glow
Gliding through the air
Making people love each other!
And making people be friends!

Fearne Bottomley (7)
Mapplewells Primary & Nursery School, Sutton-In-Ashfield

Wild Rivers

A kennings

Wild-whoosher
Speedy-smasher
Bubble-blower
Sea-swooper
Super-sloper
Bubble-popper
Clear-crasher
Life-giver
Windy-whoosher
Water coming from north
Going past the wild plants.

Jennifer Marsh (8)
Mapplewells Primary & Nursery School, Sutton-In-Ashfield

Aphrodite

Pretty beauty and love
Pretty lips and hair
Pretty swans pulled her in a chariot carriage
Pretty daughter of Zeus, daughter of Zeus

She makes people fall in love
Through her white doves.

Gracie Peel (8)
Mapplewells Primary & Nursery School, Sutton-In-Ashfield

The Mighty Gods

Zeus, Zeus, the god of the gods
Lightning bolts go past everywhere
Zapping people when he's angry

Poseidon, the god of the sea
Holding his trident like me
Very proudly like me.

Jenson Sowter (7)
Mapplewells Primary & Nursery School, Sutton-In-Ashfield

Zeus

Beautiful lightning, beautiful lightning
Shining through the sky
Mighty thunderbolt shining in the sky
King of gods, terrifying to look at
The thunderbolt was coming
From Mount Olympus.

Phoebe North (7)
Mapplewells Primary & Nursery School, Sutton-In-Ashfield

Aphrodite

She's so mighty
She's so pretty
She has beautiful dove's
As white as snow
And her hair is everywhere
All on the floor
She is really nice
Just like rice!

Oliver Birkett (8)
Mapplewells Primary & Nursery School, Sutton-In-Ashfield

Tarnished Flower

A kennings

Murky-thrower
Life-taker
Animal-killer
Cruel-thinker
Idiotic life-crasher
Unhappy wild creature
Violent-imaginer
Life-breaker
Raining trash
Brain-looper.

Morgan Clarke (9)
Mapplewells Primary & Nursery School, Sutton-In-Ashfield

Crashing Rivers

R ivers race near rocks
I n the woods, you hear knocks
V ast rivers are very neat
E ven the fish need the meat
R apid river smashes against rocks.

Ethan Clarke (9)
Mapplewells Primary & Nursery School, Sutton-In-Ashfield

Bubbly River

Bubbly river is like normal
Only with a waterfall
That's why I write about a bubbly river
It was very fast
I would describe it like
It's as fast as a cheetah.

Lena Purczynska (9)
Mapplewells Primary & Nursery School, Sutton-In-Ashfield

Calm And Rapid Rivers

Rapid rivers race
In a big disgrace
They're not a straight line
You can search that online
And have a good time
To the rhyme that takes time
For the crime.

Jasmine Hopkinson (8)
Mapplewells Primary & Nursery School, Sutton-In-Ashfield

Ares

He has two symbols
The dog and vulture
The god of war, he is a torturer
He was a bloody spear
Dived at his enemies
He has a helper to
Fight with his armies.

Jackson Walker (7)
Mapplewells Primary & Nursery School, Sutton-In-Ashfield

Rocky Rivers

A rocky river is a rocky road but just wet and wild
The fast river smacked into the rocks
When it's calm people swim in it with their child
People fish in it on docks.

Archie Harland (8)
Mapplewells Primary & Nursery School, Sutton-In-Ashfield

Hera

Beautiful flowers
Wonderful clothes
Beautiful shoes
Wonderful eyes and nose

Goddess of home
And marriage
Perfect peacocks
Beside her carriage.

Megan Fallows (8)
Mapplewells Primary & Nursery School, Sutton-In-Ashfield

Apollo

Loved to play music
On his golden lyre
Helped him create poetry and art

Art, beautiful as the sun
Music as relaxing as a bath
Poetry, amazing as a star.

Harry Stephen Beardsley (8)
Mapplewells Primary & Nursery School, Sutton-In-Ashfield

Aphrodite

Amazing Aphrodite
Lovely lady of love
Beautiful birds carried her carriage
Two doves bring marriage.

Lexi Stainsby (7)
Mapplewells Primary & Nursery School, Sutton-In-Ashfield

Minecraft

Square people
Ender dragons
Purple-eyed
Mineshaft
Green grass
Grey stone
Lava lakes
TNT explosions
Humongous holes
Super-flat
Square suns
Marvellous moons
Hot furnaces
Cold lakes
Swimming drowned
Hard obsidian
Indestructible bedrock
Nice nights
Very peaceful
Accelerating Adex
Bright sea lantern

Spotty cows
Shining stars
Blobby fish
Silly squid
Porky pigs
Honeybees
Funny chickens
Beefy cows
Big houses
Silly villagers
Mine diamonds
Tamed dogs
Stray cats
Iron ore
Trading stuff
Blue beds
Wild withers
Rock blocks
Baking cakes
Mild mines
Gold ingots
Pointy mountain

Giant games
Lovely build
Minecraft rails
Dragonflies
Armour stand
Sugarcane
Turquoise turtles
Comfortable beds
Slithery snakes
Bad mobs
Fun mods
Diamond ores
Apple trees
Large landscapes
Small saplings
White quartz
Name tags
Farm fields
Crazy crabs
Funny friends
Spruce trees
Birth trees

Woodlands
Woolly sheep
Red wool
Grey wool
Rainbows
Lime wool
Iron golem
Red roses
Water bucket
Mini-games
Creamy milk
Big battles
Throwing snowballs
Window glass
Black wool
Multicolours
Lovely hearts
Green leaves
Oak leaves
Farming wheat
Sandstone
Northern lights

Oak stairs
Redstone
Red powder.

Dylan McElwaine (10)
Moat Primary School, Castle Balfour Demesne, Lisnaskea

Everyday Farming

I wake up in the morning to the sound of the cows mooing
When I get out, I check that all the cows are okay,
I throw in bedding straw to the cows and calves
I give silage to them too,
And make sure their water is clean to drink.
I hop into the John Deere 6400 and stack her up!
She is green as grass
Get the bucket filled with silage
The cattle are going crazy for the sweet smell of it!
I dump it at their big, red noses
Job done, let's do something else
Let's go to the other Deere and fire her up!
Hook on the lime spreader
Now let's get lime spreading!
That stuff is white as can be
I've spread 200 tonnes
Now time for sleep, I'm knackered.

Mackenzie Wilson (10)
Moat Primary School, Castle Balfour Demesne, Lisnaskea

World War

W icked scars from the soldiers in the war
O h, such awful food they had to eat, yuck! It smelt like feet
R aggy clothes they had to wear but they always tear
L ots of tanks ready for war
D iseases going around from rats, men white as ghosts

W omen had to look after the farms when they left
A rmed soldiers ready to fight
R ats running through trenches.

Max Hogg (10)
Moat Primary School, Castle Balfour Demesne, Lisnaskea

Kittens

K ittens are the cutest
I love the golden ones, they're the best
T hey come in ginger, golden, black and brown
and other colours too
T hough if you see a dark black cat, they say it
brings good luck
E ven though they're cute, they may be
dangerous too
N ips and scratches you can get
S o if you see a cat or kitten, beware.

Ella Kerr (9)
Moat Primary School, Castle Balfour Demesne, Lisnaskea

Kinder

K inder chocolate is so yummy
I t is yummy in my tummy
N ice to eat, it is so sweet
D elicious to eat, just like meat
E xciting to taste
R unning the race.

Katie Rusk (9)
Moat Primary School, Castle Balfour Demesne, Lisnaskea

Space Police

There are criminals in space
That steal with lots of grace
They push and barge
As if they were the crazy people
Who were always put in charge.

People are always reporting
So police are currently hunting
Space is never really in peace
So this is why we have our
Amazing space police!

They are now flying
Whilst thieves are really trying
To stay out of sight
As for the brave space police
They are always ready to fight!

Elena Mouratidou (9)
New Hall Primary & Children's Centre, Sutton Coldfield

Fantastic Family

When you need them, they're always there,
When I need to talk, they find time to spare,
Unlike friends that come and go,
Your family is the best you'll know,
When I'm low and feeling down,
I love my mum because she's always around,
She always cares and loves me.

Louise Rowan (9)
New Hall Primary & Children's Centre, Sutton Coldfield

In A Galaxy Far Far Away

In a galaxy far far away
It is not like a usual day
It is dull, it is dark
So the poor alien children cannot go to the park
So the little aliens have to make their fun another way
They play hide-and-seek and chase each other away
When they eat, it is not much fun
Because all of the crops get burnt by the sun
In a galaxy, far far away
There are living creatures and they want to play
These creatures are not like you and me
Because they do not have toys and what we eat
Even though we are different in many ways
We can all be friends at the end of the day.

Gracie Fryer (8)
St Ann's CE Primary School, Rainhill

Through The Bedroom Door

Ten lazy children, ready to dine,
One passed out, then there were nine.

Nine lazy children, a bit overweight,
One went to the cinema, then there were eight.

Eight lazy children, all aged eleven,
One left to see her mate, then there were seven.

Seven lazy children, who like Twix,
One went to the hospital, then there were six.

Six lazy children, barely alive,
One did a colossal sneeze, then there were five.

Five lazy children, who act poor,
One went on holiday, then there were four.

Four lazy children, afraid of a bee,
One got stung, then there were three.

Three lazy children, one needed the loo,
Accidentally went themself, then there were two.

Two lazy children, the others were gone,
Another kid left, then there was one.

One lazy child, eating a scone,
They choked on a raisin, then there were none.

Natalie Byrne (9)
St Ann's CE Primary School, Rainhill

Dare To Be Different

Dare to be different,
It's easy to do,
The world would be boring,
With 10,000 of you.

Dare to be different,
Don't be told who to love,
Respect others' beliefs,
God or no God above.

Dare to be different,
Don't choose to tolerate,
Uniqueness is beautiful,
We should always celebrate.

Dare to be different,
Follow your own star,
Enough of the fakery,
Just be who you are.

Dare to be different,
Let your weirdness shine,
Be brave and be bold,
Stand out in the line.

Dare to be different,
Don't try to fit in,
If you try to be normal,
You will never ever win.

Alice Bonney (8)

St Ann's CE Primary School, Rainhill

Forever Friends

Friends are precious, honest and true,
Friends are the ones to turn to when you're feeling blue,
They are amazing, fantastic and wonderfully kind,
They are who I turn to when I'm out of my mind,
If outside, it's rain or shine,
I'm so glad that you are mine,
I love you every day and night,
Because you make my life feel bright,
I'll keep you safe inside my heart
And my friend, I will never let us part.

Amie Macdonald (8)
St Ann's CE Primary School, Rainhill

The Rescue Dog

The dog in the park is a big disgrace,
The dog in the park is a bit misplaced,
The dog in the park is a big, poor dog,
The dog in the park had to open the door!
The dog in the park needed some love,
The dog in the park finally found his hug,
The rescue dog was no longer in the park,
The rescue dog had a little bark,
And the rescue dog had a big rest before it got dark.

Jessica Sparkes (8)
St Ann's CE Primary School, Rainhill

The Planets

Mercury is so hot,
It's closest to the sun,
If you went on holiday there,
It wouldn't be much fun.

Venus is the brightest,
The brightest by far,
So bright it has a nickname,
Which is 'Morning Star'.

There are eight planets
One of them is Mars
But all we can see from Earth
Are the shining stars.

Alfie Lowry (9)
St Ann's CE Primary School, Rainhill

My Nanny, Ann

My nanny, Ann, might not know who I am,
My nanny, Ann, might not remember my name,
But I can remember the games that we played.

Dementia is cruel, dementia is tough
But my nanny, Ann, is more than enough.

My nanny, Ann, likes to sing and dance,
She likes to play with her doll's golden hair
While she sits in her chair.

Bella-Rose Jones (9)
St Ann's CE Primary School, Rainhill

Imagine The Unbelievable!

Imagine if money was no value,
Because it floated into the sky,
So take a deep breath, take it in,
Imagine what you'd buy!

A black hole sucked up prices,
Because happiness is always a treat,
So grab your spacesuits and helmets,
Because this is going to be sweet!

Ella Roberts (9)
St Ann's CE Primary School, Rainhill

Space

Whoosh! There I go into space,
Thinking about the adventures to come,
Below me, I hear my friends and family scream with excitement,
Zoom! I am in the murky, dim-lit space,
I can't believe my eyes, wow!
The infinite space is like a never-ending tunnel,
As I see the azure, emerald Earth from afar, it looks magnificent,
The cosmic, starry night sky is like pixie dust fluttering down from the sky,
Boom! There I am, back in my warm, cosy bed
Wondering if it is all just a dream.

Emily Carlin (11)
St Bartholomew's CE Primary School, West Pinchbeck

The Secrets Of Space

The eerie silence in space,
Makes my heart race and race,
All the comets shooting by,
As I uncertainly swim and fly.

The sun's blistering surface,
Smiles with caring kindness,
Whoosh, a golden shooting star,
Travelling from afar,
I then turn my head,
To see a silver, rocky bed.

Mercury, I think,
The beauty makes me blink,
Venus is a wonder,
Its greenhouse gas makes a lot of thunder,
Earth's emerald, fresh ground,
With a blanket of azure all around,
Ah, here is Mars
But not the chocolate bars,
Next is the giant of them all,
Jupiter and it sixty-seven moons,

Saturn is like a ring around a finger,
Never wanting to linger.

So close to the end, here is Uranus
Some wild winds and a turquoise surface,
Last is the furthest of them all,
Neptune, a cobalt, smooth beach ball.

Space is one thing,
Amazing if you have seen
All of the planets,
Live in secret!

Amber Nieburg (11)
St Bartholomew's CE Primary School, West Pinchbeck

One Hungry Mouth

I'm a dark hoover, sucking up space,
I'm a colossal mouth, hungry for planets,
I'm a blackened hula hoop, rotating in circles,
I'm an African man's belly button, coiled into a circle,
I'm a car tyre covered in oozy, black tar,
I'm a wagon's spinning wheel,
I'm eternal darkness, inflicting horror,
I'm a beaten boy's eye, black and blue,
I'm an endless pit, consuming anything and everything,
I'm a...
Black hole.

Harry Slack (10)
St Bartholomew's CE Primary School, West Pinchbeck

A Journey Into Space

I was going into the incredible galaxy,
I was admiring the planets very gratefully,
I looked in awe at the amazing space,
I had a gigantic smile upon my face,
I then saw the planets, oh yes, they were beautiful,
I saw them all, so many, they were multiple,
I wondered which one was my favourite, I was sure I couldn't pick,
I then decided on the moon, because it was so cosmic.

Ava Judkins (9)
St Bartholomew's CE Primary School, West Pinchbeck

The Solar System

Mercury is a ball of rock floating near the sun,
Venus is a flaming balloon thrown to the sky,
Earth is an azure orb floating in ecstasy,
Mars is a red beach ball floating in a pool,
Jupiter is a marble, rolling on tarmac,
Saturn is a basketball, thrown through a hoop,
Uranus is a frisbee thrown into space,
Neptune is a crystal ball showing the sea.

Gwilym Gough (10)
St Bartholomew's CE Primary School, West Pinchbeck

The Earth

Earth is like a cloud of land and water floating in space,
Earth is like a blue and green beach ball,
Earth is like a sphere rotating around the sun,
The Earth is like a spinning two pence coin,
The Earth is like an eye peeking out of an ebony curtain,
Earth is like a gigantic blueberry swimming in a pitch-black pool.

Poppy Payne (9)
St Bartholomew's CE Primary School, West Pinchbeck

Life On Mars

Bang!
That's the sound of the storm,
The deadly, dangerous storm,
This is Mars,
Mars is like the Earth's sister,
The uninhabited planet is 250,000 miles away,
Mars is like a red ball floating in a black pool,
Mars is like a strawberry ice cream,
In a dark chocolate ice cream cone.

Archie Pattinson (11)
St Bartholomew's CE Primary School, West Pinchbeck

Earth

The Earth is a beach ball floating in the air,
The Earth is a gigantic sphere,
The Earth is an azure blue balloon,
The Earth is a magnificent ball of water,
The Earth is two, glossy, clean bowls glued together,
The Earth is spray-painted blue,
The Earth is an eyeball, peeking through black curtains.

Charlie Hibbard (11)
St Bartholomew's CE Primary School, West Pinchbeck

Planet Nine

Is there any oxygen?
Is it mysterious?
Is it a star or a planet?
We do not know.

Is it real?
Is it alive?
Are they any aliens on it?
We do not know.

Are there any materials to use?
Is there any food?
Is it called Planet Nine?
When will we know?

Evie-Mai Walton (10)
St Bartholomew's CE Primary School, West Pinchbeck

Jupiter

Jupiter is as hard as nails
Jupiter is like a huge beach ball
Jupiter is as round as an orange
Jupiter is like a large rock spinning slowly
Jupiter is as dark as chocolate
Jupiter is an airless planet
Jupiter is as cosmic as Saturn.

Sophie Storey (9)
St Bartholomew's CE Primary School, West Pinchbeck

Saturn

Saturn, a ball aiming for the hoop,
Saturn, a ball with a hula hoop,
Saturn, a ball with a road,
Saturn, a ball with a ring,
Saturn, a globe with golden sand,
Saturn, a golden egg.

Samuel Start (10)
St Bartholomew's CE Primary School, West Pinchbeck

The Sun

The sun is a hot ball of fire
The sun is orange with flames
The sun is like a golden coin in the sky
The sun is a burning, blazing thing to touch
The sun is a bright light in the sky.

Olivia Smith (9)
St Bartholomew's CE Primary School, West Pinchbeck

Monster Trouble

There once was a galactic monster named Bob and he had a job, but this job was more of a hobby because when he was hungry, he would eat part of the moon. Every day, it was *munch, crunch* and *snap!* He loved the taste of its glorious good waste. So he munched and he crunched until it was all gone. This was a scrumptious taste from the moon's waist or even its whole body. However, one day it would all end for one furry friend.
When Bob woke up, he had a sneak and ate a bubble floating around in space. After his snack, Bob travelled to work to eat all the moon.
Once he was there, he had to tackle the moon bear, but let's not talk about that So Bob got there, pulled up a floating chair and started to munch. He munched and crunched and bit, he chewed and swallowed and gulped the moon's pure beauty, it tasted even better than it looked.
However, now Bob had eaten half of the moon and felt very sick. He started to moan and groan and roll around, but in space, there's no gravity, so Bob started to really bowl into the air.

Now to this day, all the aliens say that a floating thing flies by their house and gets closer almost every day.

Joshua Medley (10)
Wakefield Methodist Junior & Infant School, Thornes

Fat Pat The Astronaut

He was extremely fat and his name was Pat
That's why he was called Fat Pat
Astronauting was his job
He always had some junk food in his gob
Up in the rocket he would (slowly) fly
But not without a burger, chips, biscuits and a pie
Some say he is large, some say he is chubby
The food in his beard was particularly grubby
He ate so much food he felt whacked
His head swelled up and his helmet cracked
The rocket was unable to start
It suddenly did when he did a fart
On the day Pat flew past Mars
He couldn't see because of all the piled up chocolate bars
Pat finally completed his mission
Even though his trump was like a nuclear fission
One day, he'll go on a diet and not be fat
That's the story of Astronaut Pat.

Reuben Kershaw (10)
Wakefield Methodist Junior & Infant School, Thornes

Cosmic Cakes

To make the perfect cake, you need to add a bit of space
Gather a million stars from around the galactic Milky Way
Steal some of Yoda's wardrobe and Darth Vader's lightsabers, make sure you don't get caught
Pinch a bit of Earth's crust, make sure not to take that much!
Mix your luminous conundrum at the speed of light

Slice and dice the darkest black holes, don't suck everything up
Set the sun to 180 degrees, try not to freeze Earth
Sprinkle some of Pluto's particles, mixed with some of Mars' finest iron
Scatter on some moon dust
With a side of bright blue moon cheese, make sure not to sneeze!

And last but not least, grab a nearby rocket speeding past
And now time to serve your cosmic cake... enjoy!

Eliza Iqbal (10)
Wakefield Methodist Junior & Infant School, Thornes

Pathetic Planets

Monstrous Mercury's got an attitude
Venomous Venus is getting quite rude
Eager Earth is running around
Mindful Mars won't let you down
Jealous Jupiter stole a roll
Sad ol' Saturn felt without a soul
Urgent Uranus jumped in a hole
Nervous Neptune soon found the galactic mole!

Now I'm floating round in space
While all the planets have a race
I'm so very confused
As my Internet gets defused
I cannot Google
Why are all these planets having such a doodle?

Isabelle Stephenson (10)
Wakefield Methodist Junior & Infant School, Thornes

Alien Invasion

The audacious aliens attacked one day
The moon which is far, far away
They thought it was a good idea
To further their alien career

They are as brave as lions
And are as fearless as a knight
And you would want them on your side when
Someone starts a fight

But what happened on the moon was
A whole different story
When the aliens attacked with all of their glory

All that was there was a block of cheese
And an American flag
Flapping in the breeze.

Margaret Morgan (10)
Wakefield Methodist Junior & Infant School, Thornes

Cosmic Cupcakes Made In Space

Crumble a cluster of comets and a shower of meteorites
Over super lava, glittering and bright

Sprinkle on some planet particles
Using a galactic grater
Mix together with a solar spoon
In the deepest Martian crater

Into your celestial concoction
Pop a star from Orion's belt
Choose a layer of ozone
Use a sunbeam to gently melt

Then mix it all together and
Serve on a flying saucer...
Eat! Enjoy.

Emma Haigh (9)
Wakefield Methodist Junior & Infant School, Thornes

Virgin Rockets To Space

Space is ace
Nothing that you would face
Richard Branson is on the case
Trying to sell his vision to visit space
He is on the moon
Hoping to sell his tickets by noon
You will go up in a rocket
That will cost you a bit out of your pocket
As you exit Earth
You will feel its every worth
Experience the curse
Then you can be the one to say you did it first.

Hassan Shahzad (9)
Wakefield Methodist Junior & Infant School, Thornes

Bob The Alien

Bob the alien fell out of space
Because an asteroid hit him right in his face
Bob the alien whizzed around the moon
Like an absolute buffoon
Bob the alien visited Mars
Always catching stars
But all he wanted was a flash car
Bob the alien buying a satellite
Ended up having a fright
Bob the alien's favourite place
Is always outer space.

Thomas Warwick (10)
Wakefield Methodist Junior & Infant School, Thornes

Is The Moon Cheese?

Is the moon made out of cheese?
I don't think so but people do believe
As I have not been there
It is yet to be seen
If the moon was made out of cheese
It could be cheddar or Brie
Earth is next to the moon
But we can't see if it is a cheese moon
Mercury, Venus and Mars can see the moon
And they pass the cheese moon
Jupiter is a jump away and Saturn is a space hopper
That is still near
But far from the cheese moon
And in the distance is Uranus
Spinning around
And Neptune is an empty ocean that can still see
The glow of the cheese moon
Pluto is the icy dwarf planet
That has a glisten from the cheese moon
We will have to wait and see.

Kenzie Kavanagh (9)
Walsden St Peter's Primary School, Walsden

All Eight Planets

Mercury, the smallest
Hotter than the rest
Closest to the sun
It really is the best

The second planet from the sun
Is named Venus, did you know?
Still too hot to live on
It will never snow

Earth, seven continents
All fascinating to see
Seventy-one percent water
But still life for you and me

Mars, the red planet
Red and rocky as can be
Earth might be destroyed one day
Could Mars be home to me?

Jupiter, the giant
Heaviest in the sky

Not sure how it stays up in space
Do you know why?

In the solar system
Saturn sits on a slant
Surrounded by rings of ice
Too cold to grow a plant

Uranus blue
Seventh planet from the sun
Three billion kilometres away
Brrr... turn the heating on

Neptune last in the solar system
Minus two hundred degrees
You could not live on this planet
You would surely freeze.

Jarrod Seville (9)
Walsden St Peter's Primary School, Walsden

Poor Old Michael Collins

Poor old Michael Collins
Sitting quietly on Apollo 11
Waiting as Neil and Buzz leap around
Looking out of the cockpit at the blackness
And the occasional flicker of a star
Houston down below roar at the success
But Michael is all alone
250,000 miles away from home

The buggy's engine whines
Michael Collins cries
"Why can't I be out there?"
In his anger, he turns the rockets on
It pulls the buggy clean away
He grins to himself, Neil and Buzz wait
The sound is engulfed by the inky blackness

Back on Earth, Buzz is mad
Poor Michael is on the run
His NASA days are over
Oh, poor Michael Collins

All alone somewhere in America
Where Buzz and Neil can't reach him.

Arthur Thomas (10)

Walsden St Peter's Primary School, Walsden

The Colourful Cartwheel

This galaxy is bright and swirling
And its beauty is still unfurling
It's a ring galaxy with a smooth, blue ring
Made of stars, dust and gas - a celestial thing
The centre is orange, reds and yellows
It creates energy like a pair of bellows

The cartwheel is 200 million years old
Quite a short time for a galaxy to mould
Formed by two galaxies colliding, we're told
The great crash was extremely powerful and bold

It is 500 million lightyears away
It develops and changes day by day
A brilliant place to test out theories
Yet we are still full of queries.

Beatrice Davis (10)
Walsden St Peter's Primary School, Walsden

Our Space Dream

In bed on a cold, wet night
Where I dreamed of a flight
For that magical trip
On an enormous spaceship

It suddenly became true!
And through the Heavens, I flew
Beamed up to a spaceship
With a jolt and a whip!
Just missing the moon
I knew outer space was coming soon
We sped past Mars
Onwards to the stars!

Through the galaxy, we travelled
That's when everything unravelled
Through a black hole, we flew
The spaceship tore in two!

I awoke with a scream
To find it was all just a dream.

Georgia Watt (10)
Walsden St Peter's Primary School, Walsden

The Little Spaceship

I am a spaceship
Blasting off to Mars
But suddenly
I crash into stars

I go tumbling through space
Dodging black holes
Falling, falling, falling
Flying past space moles

The mole stops to say hi
The expression on his face
Showed his surprise
That we were in this place

We landed on Mars
The great red zone
Felt the ground
Then thought, *let's go home.*

Charlotte Beresford (10)
Walsden St Peter's Primary School, Walsden

Acrostic Poem

S tars shone ever so bright
O ur planets slowly orbit the sun
L evitating space
A ll rotating
R unning across space

S aturn is a planet
Y ou're not gonna see it
S un shines through
T hough it may burn you
E arth is where we live
M any years to come.

Lily Jones (9)
Walsden St Peter's Primary School, Walsden

The Nine Planets

Here are nine planets that we know
Round and round the sun they go
Mercury, Venus, Earth and Mars
These are the planets near our star

Jupiter, Saturn, Uranus too
Neptune, Pluto, we can't see you
These are the nine planets that we know
Round and round the sun they go.

Ruby Chadwick (9)
Walsden St Peter's Primary School, Walsden

Apollo Mission

A ldrin
P acific landing
O rbit
L unar
L anding
O ne small step

M ichael Collins
I solation
S tars and stripes
S aturn
I nspiration
O ne giant leap!
N eil Armstrong.

Ollie Cross (9)
Walsden St Peter's Primary School, Walsden

Solar System

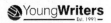

S pace
O rion
L una
A pollo
R overs

S aturn
Y uri Gagarin
S un
T itan
E xtraterrestrial
M eteor.

Max Cross (9)
Walsden St Peter's Primary School, Walsden

YOUNG WRITERS INFORMATION

We hope you have enjoyed reading this book – and that you will continue to in the coming years.

If you're a young writer who enjoys reading and creative writing, or the parent of an enthusiastic poet or story writer, do visit our website **www.youngwriters.co.uk**. Here you will find free competitions, workshops and games, as well as recommended reads, a poetry glossary and our blog. There's lots to keep budding writers motivated to write!

If you would like to order further copies of this book, or any of our other titles, then please give us a call or order via your online account.

Young Writers
Remus House
Coltsfoot Drive
Peterborough
PE2 9BF
(01733) 890066
info@youngwriters.co.uk

Join in the conversation!
Tips, news, giveaways and much more!

YoungWritersUK

@YoungWritersCW